Surprise from the Sky

written by Pam Holden
illustrated by Pauline Whimp

Nan is Charlie's Grandmother.
She lives on a small island far out in the sea.
There are no schools or roads on the island.

Charlie went on a boat to visit her.

Every day Charlie and Nan went
fishing with their friends.
They all swam in the sea.
When they were hungry,
they had lunch on the beach.

On Saturday, Nan said to Charlie, "Today we'll go to meet the plane. Paulo the pilot will fly over the sea to bring things for everybody."

"He won't bring anything for me, will he?" asked Charlie.
"You wait and see," said Nan.
"Paulo always brings something for everyone."

Everybody on the island went to wait for Paulo's plane.
Before long the people saw the plane coming closer and closer.
Paulo waved to them as he flew down to land.

Paulo got out of the plane with
letters and boxes.
He took out a big bag of sausages
for one family, and a bike for
one of the children.
There were some small plants
for Nan's garden.

There were new boots for one of the men.
Lots of things came out of the plane, but there was nothing for Charlie.

Next Paulo loaded the plane with things to take back to town. He took two bags of fish and lots of letters and boxes.

Then he put in a basket of oranges
and a sack of vegetables.

After the plane took off,
something came floating down.
Charlie ran to catch it.
It was a small parachute with a toy!

He saw more parachutes floating down.
The children ran to catch the toys.
Everybody was happy and laughing!

"See!" said Nan. "Paulo always brings something for everyone."
"I like meeting Paulo's plane," said Charlie.
"I like your island, Nan."